THE
INNKEEPER'S DAUGHTER

THE YOUNG DISCIPLES™
VOLUME 1

THE
INNKEEPER'S DAUGHTER

KATHRYN H. KIDD

HATRACK RIVER
PUBLICATIONS

Cover and interior art by Paul Mann
Cover design by James Fedor
This book was set in 18-point Glyphix Foundry "Souvienne" from
        SWFTE International, using WordPerfect 5.1 and a Hewlett-
        Packard LaserJet III. It was then reduced and printed on pH-
        neutral paper.

First printing November 1990
10 9 8 7 6 5 4 3 2 1

ISBN 0-9624049-2-6

Library of Congress 90-084682

for Emily Card —
my most important critic

Look for the next volume of
The Young Disciples™ Series
by Kathryn H. Kidd:

Rachel at the Wedding

An Angry Morning

Deborah's mother was in a bad mood. Deborah couldn't remember when she had seen her mother so angry and upset.

Usually, Mother woke the whole family with singing, as she roused everyone from the bed they all shared to do the morning's work. On those days, her mood spread from one family member to another until everyone began the day with a smile. Deborah's big sister Leah and her little sister Ruth — and even their brother Isaac — would sing or hum while they put on their sandals and got ready to begin the day.

Deborah's father didn't hum, of course. He was the father, and he had to at least act serious so everyone would know he was important. But sometimes Deborah saw him tap out the beat of a song on his thigh as he watched to make sure that the children were doing their morning chores.

Today, though, there was no singing. By the dim lamplight, Deborah saw her mother's face twisted into a scowl.

"Get *up!*" Mother scolded while everyone else was still stretching and opening their eyes. "There's too much work for you to lie in bed like rich people."

She pulled Isaac off the wooden bed by his ankle, and he fell the few inches to the floor with a *whump.*

"That hurt!" he said, rubbing his bottom in pain and surprise. At Isaac's next birthday he would be thirteen years old. Then he would be a man, and Mother couldn't pull him off the bed even when she was in a bad mood. But at twelve, he was still a boy. And today, no one was safe from Mother's anger.

"Then you should have gotten up when I told you to," Mother said. "You have work to do. Don't you hear the animals in the yard down below? They need to be milked and watered and fed."

"I know what to do." Now Isaac was grumpy, too. "I feed the animals every morning, don't I?" Hurriedly, he tied a girdle around the waist of his tunic, the robe that boys and girls and men and women all wore both day and night. Then he left the room before Mother could say anything else. Father scurried off behind Isaac, escaping the scene in the bedroom.

As soon as the men were gone, Mother turned her anger on the girls. "Ruth, pick your girdle off the floor!" Quickly, Ruth picked up the sash that had fallen on the floor and tied it around her waist without shaking the dirt off first.

Deborah saw her mother's face twist up in anger at Ruth. Quickly, she reached down and pulled the girdle off Ruth. She slapped it against her arm to remove the dirt from the floor. Then, tenderly, she tied it around the waist of Ruth's blue tunic.

Leaning down, Deborah saw Ruth's lower lip quiver as if she were about to cry. Ruth was only five; she was too young to know that crying would only make her mother angrier. Deborah made a face at Ruth and touched the little girl's nose with her fingertip. Ruth giggled, and the crisis was over.

But today, even helping Deborah's little sister wasn't good enough to make Mother happy. Before Deborah had even straightened up, Mother barked, "Are you going to take all *day?* I can't do any work until you get the water. Go! *Now!*"

Leah and Deborah hurried to obey their mother, stopping only to pick up an earthenware jug and the goatskin water bottle that was hanging from a peg in the kitchen wall. Deborah was old enough to remember the goat whose skin made the water bottle she was carrying. He was a black billy goat named Nubia who had been Deborah's pet until the day Father killed him for a feast day meal.

Now Deborah had a new pet goat, but she still remembered how Father had peeled off Nubia's skin in one piece and made it into a watertight bottle. Today Deborah chose the goatskin bottle because it was lighter and easier to carry than the heavy earthenware jug that Leah balanced on her head.

Leah was thirteen years old, so she would be married within a year or two. Then Deborah would learn how to balance the earthenware jug on her own head or carry it on her hip. By then, Ruth would be old enough to carry the goatskin bottle when Deborah went to the well to get water at morning and at night.

Even though Deborah hated carrying the heavy skin of water upstairs to her family's house, she was luckier than most girls her age. Most girls had to go to the town well and wait in line until everyone else ahead of them was finished filling their jugs and skins with water. Then they had to carry the heavy water home through the narrow streets of Bethlehem. Often they had to make the long trip to the well twice a day or even three times a day.

But Deborah's father was Bethlehem's innkeeper, and Deborah and her family lived in the inn. Deborah's family and the inn's guests lived upstairs, above a courtyard where all the animals were kept. Because the animals had to be fed and watered, the inn had its own well. Deborah and Leah only had to walk down the stairs to fill their jugs and skins with water. Then they had to carry the water up the stairs again.

As soon as Leah and Deborah were out of their mother's sight, Leah breathed a sigh of relief.

"Mother is being horrible today," she said to Deborah, "and I'm afraid things are only going to get worse."

"Do all women get like this when they're expecting a baby?" Deborah asked.

Leah only shook her head. "I don't think the baby is the problem," she said. "Mother has been expecting a baby for months and months, and she's never acted like this before."

Deborah nodded solemnly. Mother had never been as cross as she was today. "If it's not the baby, then, what's wrong?" she asked, shifting the goatskin bottle from one hand to the other.

"It's the Census. The Census has everyone upset. Haven't you noticed?"

Now that she thought about it, Deborah realized that everyone *had* been nervous and edgy lately. "I don't even know what the Census is," she said, "but if it makes everyone so mad all the time, I don't think we should have one."

"We don't have a choice," Leah said. "The Romans have ordered us to count everyone who lives in the country. That's what a Census is — when everyone is counted and their names are written down."

"Why do the Romans want *that?*" Deborah asked, shaking her head. The Romans were always making extra work for people. Nobody liked the Romans.

"It's because of money and taxes," Leah said. "If a person can prove what city he was born in, he'll only have to pay half the taxes that he would otherwise."

Deborah and Leah walked through the courtyard to the well. They had to watch every step, because there were animals everywhere. There were also people sleeping in blankets on the hard ground, right next to their animals. It was still dark, and most of the people and their animals were still asleep.

When she and Leah got to the well, they sat on the edge and rested for a moment. Finally Deborah said, "If people will pay less tax after a Census, why does the Census make everyone so upset?"

"I think I'd rather pay more tax money and not have the Romans know my name and where I lived," Leah said. "Nothing good ever came from the Romans."

Deborah nodded her head in agreement, but she didn't know much about the Romans. All she knew was that Father said they were bad people. Whatever Father said, Deborah believed.

"There are other reasons people don't like the Census," Leah continued. "I think the main one is that important people can be counted wherever they live. People that the Romans don't like — and that includes us Jews — have to travel to the city where they were born to be counted. Sometimes they have to travel for days and days before they get there."

"*I* think traveling would be fun," Deborah said.

Leah only shook her head. "That's because you've never done it. Once you get away from the city, the roads are so bad that it's easy to get lost. And the girls have to walk everywhere, too. Only the boys and men get to ride."

"That's not fair!" Deborah said.

"Maybe it isn't fair, but that's the way things have always been done," Leah said. "If there's only one donkey in a family, the husband rides it. If there are two donkeys, the oldest son rides the second one."

"Then I'll just have to marry a rich man," Deborah said stubbornly. "I won't get married unless my husband has enough money to buy a donkey for everyone in the family."

Leah laughed, but she shook her head at the same time. "Walking isn't even the worst thing about traveling," she said.

"There are *worse* things?" Deborah asked. Suddenly, traveling didn't seem as fun as she had thought it would be.

"There are bears and lions that can kill you if you're not careful. And at night, you can be robbed and murdered right in the inn where you're staying."

That made Deborah angry. "No one was ever robbed or killed at *our* inn," she said hotly.

"That's because Father is careful about who he lets stay with us. Even so — whenever we have guests, Father sleeps with one eye open."

"I guess that's true," Deborah agreed. "But you haven't explained why Mother is so upset. We were born right in Bethlehem, so we don't have to travel anywhere. And since we have more guests now, we're making lots of money."

"We have too *many* guests," Leah said. "The guestrooms are filled. In all my life, I've never seen people sleeping here in the courtyard, with the animals. *Look* at them!" she said, shaking her head in amazement. "They're all curled up on the ground with the camels and the goats."

Deborah nodded solemnly. The people were all crowded together with their animals like Noah's family on the Ark. Deborah was glad she had made it through the courtyard without stepping on a hand or a foot.

"Mother has to make sure all those people are fed, and all their animals are fed and cared for," Leah continued. "And she always has to worry about robbers. This isn't a good time for her, Deborah. The best thing we can do is help her when she needs it and stay out of her way the rest of the time. Look! The sun's coming up. It's going to be a beautiful day."

Deborah looked up toward the hills surrounding the Bethlehem walls. She saw a shepherd herding the sheep down toward the city gate, and she wondered if that shepherd was Andrew. Andrew was Isaac's best friend, so Deborah knew him well. In fact, Deborah had a secret about Andrew. Even though he was only a slave, she knew that she wanted to marry him when he earned his freedom and went home to the village of Cana.

Breakfast and Boasting

When Deborah and Leah returned upstairs with their water, Mother had breakfast ready for them at the table. One by one, Mother poured running water from the goatskin over everyone's hands to wash them. That was the first part of the prayer before the meal.

The second part of prayer consisted of the actual words that were said. All together, the family members said the prayer:

> *"Blessed art Thou, Jehovah our God,*
> *King of the World, who causes to*
> *come forth bread from the earth."*

When the prayer was finished, the family sat around the table to eat the morning meal. Most of Deborah's friends ate breakfast by the handful, wrapping olives or cheese or dried fruit in a piece of bread and eating it as they did their morning chores. But because Deborah's family lived in the inn, their breakfast was bigger.

Deborah's mother had to prepare a more elaborate meal for the guests who were paying for their food.

There were olives and cheese *and* dried fruit, which were eaten with flatbread that Leah and Deborah had bought at market on the day before. There was also yogurt, made from the milk of whichever inn animals were currently producing milk.

Usually there was honey, too. Leah and Deborah had made the honey themselves, by boiling grape juice until it became thick and syrupy. They spread the honey on bread, trying not to get the purple goo on their clothes or their faces as they ate.

While the family was eating, Isaac's friend Andrew arrived with the family's sheep and goats. Deborah smiled when she heard the bleats of the animals as Andrew herded them into the little cave on the hillside underneath the inn.

Andrew always visited the inn last, because he could count on Deborah's mother to feed him breakfast with the family. Deborah often thought that Mother liked Andrew more than she liked her own children. Sure enough, when Andrew peeked inside the kitchen, Mother's lips turned up in a half-smile.

"Come on in," Mother said, sounding less grumpy than she had all day. "I might as well feed one more mouth, with this crowd we're taking care of." Carefully, balancing her stomach in front of her, she lifted herself from the chair to hold the goatskin bottle over Andrew's hands, washing them so he could eat with the family. Andrew smiled his thanks. Then, while the family waited quietly, he prayed aloud over the food before he sat down to eat.

Andrew tore off a piece of bread and spread it with honey. Then he put a slab of cheese inside the honeyed bread and took a hearty bite.

"You should see the city from the hills!" he exclaimed, when he finally swallowed. "There must be hundreds of people here. The Romans have set up big tents outside the main gate, and people are camped all over the hillside."

"That's true," Father said. "The Romans came here before they set up the tents. The captain asked where the best site for a camp would be, and we talked for a long time. Nobody makes camp around here without talking to the innkeeper first."

Father puffed out his chest importantly. He reached across the table and tore off another bit of bread. He spread it with chopped olives and took a healthy bite. Then he wiped olive oil from his lips with the knuckle of a finger and sucked the oil from his knuckle with a loud smacking sound.

"In fact," Father continued, "the Romans have filled our inn for us. Every person coming to Bethlehem for the Census stops at the tent city first. The Romans have sent the important people here."

"And the sick people," Mother said. "Don't forget the sick people. Our inn is full to bursting with the old and the sick people, as well as the important ones."

"I can see," said Andrew. "I've never seen people staying in a courtyard before now. There are so many people and animals for you to feed, it's no wonder you look so tired."

Deborah blushed. Most people didn't notice how hard women worked, and *nobody* paid attention when a woman looked tired. Nobody but Andrew. No wonder Mother liked him so much!

"The Census is hard on all of us," Father said, taking the attention away from Mother.

"I know it is," Andrew replied. "I hate the Census most of all. The Census means taxes, and my parents had to sell me into slavery for seven years to pay their taxes. When I earn my freedom — three years and two months and fourteen days from now —, I'm going straight home to Cana to claim my inheritance. Then, when the next Census comes, I'll already be at my birthplace. Then I won't have to travel anywhere."

"Will you be a slave in Cana?" Ruth asked. She always stood next to Andrew when he came to visit. Everyone knew that she had a crush on him.

"Of course not, little one," Andrew said, laughing. "Now that I've seen the world, I have big plans. When I earn my freedom, I won't be a slave *or* a shepherd. I'll take the olives and the olive oil from my family's grove and trade them for fish in Capernaum. I'll be a trader and a merchant and a rich man, too. Just you wait and see!"

Isaac rolled his eyes. "There he goes — boasting again!" he exclaimed. Then he said to Andrew, "You'll never be able to count all that money if you don't learn your numbers better."

"And you'll never learn your numbers better if you don't leave for school," Mother said. "Come over here, both of you, and wash your hands before you go."

Isaac and Andrew obediently held their hands under the running water that Mother poured from the goatskin bottle. Then each of them reached down and brought the tail of his tunic up between his legs. Then they tucked the cloth inside their girdles, freeing their legs for the run down the hill to school. That was called *girding your loins,* and Deborah had always wanted to do it.

"I wish I could gird *my* loins like that," she said as the boys ran down the stairs and off to school. "I'd run faster than a lion."

"Silly!" As soon as Andrew was gone, Mother looked cross again. "Why would a girl want to run?" Without waiting for an answer, she added, "You and Leah had better hurry to market before all the travelers get there. I want eighteen loaves of barley bread for our guests, and two loaves of wheat bread for us. Buy some olive oil and some leeks, too; and be sure to bring back some wine. Come! Wash your hands and go."

After everyone had washed, Mother took some coins from a small clay jar on a shelf and gave them to Leah. Obediently, the two girls walked down the lane to the city gate, where the merchants were set up to do their daily business. With every step she took, Deborah pretended she had girded up her own loins and was running as fast as Andrew and Isaac had run down the hill minutes before.

"Slow down!" Leah cried. "You're not a deer!"

Deborah looked above her and saw Leah standing fifty paces above her on the hill. Her hands were on her hips and she looked annoyed.

"I'm sorry," Deborah said. "I was dreaming I could run just like the boys do."

Leah's lips melted into a smile. "I used to dream that dream," she said. "In my dreams, I was a hawk who flew faster than all of them. Wait for me, and we'll pretend we're flying all the way to market."

Deborah waited patiently for her older sister to catch up to her. Even though Leah was a grown woman, ready for marriage, sometimes she could remember what it was like to be a little girl.

Those were the times when Deborah loved her most of all.

Bread and Mischief

When Leah got to the city's gate, they hurried to the stall that was run by Solomon the Breadmaker. He was the best baker in the city, and Mother had taught Leah and Deborah to visit his stall first.

When they reached the baker's stall, though, they didn't see any cakes of wheat bread or barley bread, or the rounds of flatbread that were so good when they were spread with honey. Only a lingering smell of yeast told Deborah that there had ever been bread in Solomon's stall. Solomon was busily packing to go home.

"Excuse me," said Leah. "Where is the bread? Didn't you bake any bread today?"

"Did I bake bread?" Solomon always answered one question with another one. "All night I was up baking bread. As soon as the city gate opened, customers bought every loaf I had. Let me tell you, I could have

sold a hundred loaves more. Only in my dreams do I
have a day like today."

"Are the other bakers out of bread, too?" Leah
asked.

"Are they out of bread?" Solomon replied. "Every
baker in the city is out of bread. Soon the wine merchants and the cheesemakers and everyone else will be
stripped of everything they brought to market. I wish we
had the Census every day."

"From your mouth to God's ears," said the man in
the next stall. He was Benjamin, the olive merchant.
Like Solomon, he was packing his donkey to go home.
"I only have three more flasks of olive oil left, and all my
olives are gone. If every day were as good as this one,
I could buy two more olive groves and live like a rich
man."

"We'll buy some of your olive oil," Deborah said
quickly. She wanted to make sure that she and Leah
came home with at least some of the groceries Mother
wanted.

Deborah waited while Leah bargained with Benjamin for a good price on the olive oil. Then, carrying the
flask of oil, she followed Leah to the wine merchant's
stall to buy two skins of wine. They bought a handful of
leeks, too. Then they carried their treasures up the hill
to the inn carefully, walking slowly under the heavy
weight.

When they reached the inn, Mother didn't thank
them for the groceries they had brought home. All she
said was, "Where is the bread? I sent you to get twenty
loaves."

"There is no bread," Leah said. "The travelers camped outside the city gate have bought it all. There is no bread to be bought in all of Bethlehem."

Mother put a hand on each side of her heavy stomach and groaned. "With no bread, how will we feed our guests?" she asked angrily. "If you had gone to market earlier, there would have been bread."

Deborah opened her mouth to protest, but Leah put a hand on her shoulder to silence her.

"We'll *make* bread, Mother," Leah said. "Deborah and I will do it."

"And how will you do that?" Mother snapped. "For every loaf of bread you make, you need a pinch of day-old dough to use as a starter. I don't have twenty pinches of day-old dough, and I can see that you didn't bring any dough from market."

Guiltily, Leah looked at the floor.

"I was right," Mother said. "Deborah, you go down to Solomon the Breadmaker's house and buy enough day-old dough to make twenty loaves. Hurry! And be sure you get a good price."

She put a coin in Deborah's hand and pushed her out the door.

Deborah was glad to be going into town again and away from her mother. She didn't know what was wrong with Mother, but it wasn't fair for Mother to blame everything on her children. Deborah sighed and walked down the hill as fast as she could travel in her long tunic and sandals. She pretended she was a hawk, flying down the hill to look for prey.

All of a sudden, Deborah tumbled to the ground and sprawled on the dusty narrow street. Something had tripped her, but it wasn't a rock, and it wasn't a hole. She had fallen over something that moved. She sat up and looked around to see what had caused her to fall. All she could see was a man's sandal, attached to a man's large foot.

Then Deborah heard the laughter. She looked up at the owner of the sandal and saw a Roman soldier looking down at her, laughing and making fun of her. Quickly, she stood. Without even dusting herself off, she looked up at the man and said, "You tripped me!"

The Roman soldier didn't even deny it. "You fell over my foot," he said. "Besides, you were going so fast you needed to be tripped. You're dressed like a girl, but you run like a boy."

Deborah ignored the rude soldier. She fell to her knees and found the coin she had dropped when she fell. Then, without another word, she stood and walked primly down the street. She heard the Roman soldier laughing behind her, but she ignored him as she went on her way.

Because Deborah knew better than to argue with a Roman soldier, she needed someone else to blame for her problems. This is all Mother's fault! she thought. All day long, Mother has been cranky and mean. From the moment we got out of bed, Mother has blamed everything on me. It's not fair! No — it's not *fair*.

By the time Deborah reached the home of Solomon the Breadmaker, she was ready for more bad luck. Solomon wouldn't sell day-old dough to Deborah. He said he needed it for himself.

"Why should I sell you the dough for one coin, when I can make twenty loaves of bread with it and sell that for twenty coins?" he asked. "I need every scrap of dough I can get, so I'll have extra bread for tomorrow.

I'll make a bargain with you — if you can find some day-old dough, anywhere in Bethlehem, I'll buy it from *you.*"

When Solomon said that, Deborah knew she didn't have a chance of finding any day-old dough in the city. But she also knew that her mother would be furious if she went home without any dough at all.

Deborah thought for a few moments, trying to decide what to do. Finally she said, "If I can't buy any day-old dough from you, will you make a fresh loaf of dough for me to take home now?"

"Why do you want that?" Solomon asked. "You can't cook with it. The dough won't be ready to make more bread until tomorrow."

"I know that," Deborah said. Then she lied: "I want to take it home today so we can bake bread tomorrow morning. That way, we'll have bread at the inn even if all the bread at the market is gone."

"I see," Solomon said. "In that case, I'll sell you the dough. Wait for a few minutes, and I'll make some dough for you."

Deborah sat on a mat on the floor while the baker made his fresh dough. She inspected her elbows and knees to see if she had been injured when the Roman soldier tripped her. She was almost pleased to see a small spot of blood on her right knee, where she had been scraped in the fall. Father was right: Romans were bad people. Anyone who hurt someone else on purpose couldn't be a good person.

Finally Solomon handed Deborah a fresh loaf of dough, wrapped in a damp cloth to keep it wet.

"I'll return the cloth tomorrow," Deborah said.

"Of course you will. Now, go on your way. And be sure to tell your mother that the dough is fresh. She can't use this dough as yeast until tomorrow."

"I'll do that," Deborah said, but she blushed red because she knew she was telling a lie. If Mother wanted day-old dough, Deborah would give her day-old dough. It wouldn't be Deborah's fault if the dough didn't make the other loaves of bread rise.

In fact, it would serve Mother right if all twenty new loaves of bread were ruined.

Apologies

Before Deborah walked in the front door of the inn, she started limping on her right leg. She favored her leg just a little, hoping that Mother would notice she had been hurt. If Mother felt sorry for Deborah, maybe things would be better between them.

But Mother didn't notice Deborah's limp. Without even looking up from her sewing, she said, "At last you're back! Find Leah and get to work making bread for supper." She didn't even say thank you to Deborah, although Deborah had walked down to the city twice in one morning.

Feeling sorry for herself, Deborah sighed. But soon she forgot her worries, as she and Leah set about the task of making twenty loaves of bread for the inn.

Leah put the wheat grinder on a square of clean cloth on the kitchen table. She turned the mill stones with a handle, letting Deborah do the easier job of dropping grains of wheat into the mill to be ground. Deborah liked to hear the swishing sound of the mill-stones grinding against each other as the wheat was crushed into flour.

When there was a large pile of flour on the cloth, Deborah and Leah transferred it to a large bowl. There it was mixed with water to form a big lump of dough.

"Now comes the important part," said Leah. "We'll add the day-old dough to our new dough. Then we can take our midday rest while the old dough makes the new dough rise."

Deborah felt guilty as she watched her older sister mix the "old" dough in with the new. Quickly, she prayed that somehow the dough she had purchased from Solomon the Breadmaker would work on the dough that she and Leah had just made. But even as she said the prayer, she knew God wouldn't listen to her. God didn't answer wicked prayers.

Sure enough, Deborah was awakened from her midday nap by a cry of anger from the kitchen. "The dough didn't rise!" Mother cried. "Leah, don't you know how to make bread?"

Deborah put on her sandals and went to the kitchen, where she saw Leah standing in tears next to the oven. "I did everything right, Mother," Leah said. "I've been making bread for years."

"Then Solomon the Breadmaker sold us fresh dough and pretended it was day-old," Mother said. "David!" she called, summoning Father to the kitchen. "Come see how Solomon the Breadmaker has cheated us."

When Deborah saw the dark look on Father's face, she knew things had gone horribly wrong. She hadn't realized that Mother would blame Leah, and then

Solomon the Breadmaker, if the dough didn't rise the way it should have done.

She looked from Leah's face to her mother's, and then to her father's. Father's skin was red with anger. Mother's anger showed in the tears on her face. The tears that Leah shed were tears of embarrassment and shame.

Taking a deep breath for strength, Deborah said quietly, "I did it." But nobody heard her. She had to say it louder: "*I* did it."

"What did you do?" Father asked.

"I made the bread go bad," Deborah said. And then, before she lost her courage, she told her family all the things that had happened during the day — how hurt she felt when Mother snapped at her, and how angry she felt when the Roman soldier laughed when she fell. She told how Solomon the Breadmaker didn't have any day-old dough to sell, but he sold her new dough after she promised not to use it for leavening until the following day.

"Why didn't you tell us?" Father asked. "Solomon the Breadmaker would have sold us twenty new loaves of dough, and we could have baked them into twenty good loaves of bread. Now, after all our work, our twenty loaves of bread are ruined."

"I didn't think of that," Deborah said miserably. "All I thought was how angry Mother would be if I came home without any day-old dough."

"We're not angry about the dough," said Father, "but we're disappointed because you lied to us. Haven't we taught you not to lie?"

Deborah hung her head. She *had* been taught, time and time again, that lying was almost the worst thing a person could do. Telling the truth was so important that God had made it one of the Ten Commandments. Deborah had broken that commandment. Now her parents would never trust her again.

Finally she spoke. "Today, when the Roman soldier tripped me, I thought he was a terrible person. I said to myself that nobody who was good would ever hurt anyone else on purpose. Now, in the same day, I've hurt all of you. I'm sorry."

Father put his arm around Deborah's shoulder. "Don't worry about the Roman soldier," he said. "When the Savior comes, He'll crush the people who oppress us. Then the Romans will never bother us again.

"But you *do* need to worry about yourself," Father continued. "We need to make a world where the Savior will be welcome. We need to follow all the Ten Commandments and do everything we can to get ready for the Savior's birth."

Deborah turned to her mother. "Mother, I'm sorry," she said.

"I'm sorry, too," Mother said. "I'm sorry I was so cross with you that you felt trapped into lying. I'm also sorry that we have no bread to serve our guests for dinner. We'll have to make a dinner that is so good our guests won't miss the bread."

"I'll make the dinner," Deborah said.

"I'll help you," said Leah. "I know how hard it is to admit the truth once you've made a mistake."

"When did you make a mistake as bad as this one?" asked Deborah.

Leah chewed her lip as she thought for a moment. "I don't know," she finally admitted, "but I'm sure I've done something wrong *sometime*."

Mother went upstairs to spin some wool into yarn, and Father walked down the hill to see how many travelers were staying at the Romans' tent city. Soon Deborah and Leah were laughing and joking the way they always did, and Deborah knew that her family still loved her despite the mistake she had made.

Before the sun set, Mother had one request to make of Deborah. She asked Deborah to bake the twenty loaves of bread, just as she would have baked them if the loaves had risen the way they were supposed to have done. Deborah baked each loaf, one by one, flattening it into a long, paper-thin circle and cooking it on top of the domed oven.

When the last loaf was finished, Deborah asked her mother, "Why did you want me to cook the bread?"

"First," Mother said, "I want you to taste the bread you've made."

Deborah pulled off a bit of the unleavened bread and took a bite of it. Then she made a face as she swallowed the bite. "This is terrible!" she said to her mother. "It tastes just like Passover bread!"

"That's exactly what it is," Mother said. "Every year, when the Passover holiday reminds us how quickly the Children of Israel ran away from Egypt, we cook bread that doesn't have any yeast in it. Now you know how to make bread for Passover."

"These twenty loaves won't keep until Passover time, will they?" Deborah asked hopefully.

Mother laughed. "Of course not. But now that they're cooked, the cattle will eat them. Tear them into strips and feed them to the cows and the goats."

As Deborah tore the bread into bite-sized pieces for the cattle, she thought how smart her mother was to

have found something to do with the ruined loaves of
bread. Feeding the bread to the animals was a good
thing to do with it. Unless it was Passover, only cattle
would eat food that was so tasteless and dead.

Uninvited Guests

Dinnertime was a busy time for Deborah and her family. The inn's guests gathered around the dinner table, talking and eating in shifts while Mother and Leah and Deborah fed them. The inn had chairs and tables and beds, just like a rich man's house. When there were guests at the inn, Deborah's family ate like a rich family, too. Sometimes there was even fish or meat.

Tonight, there was a full table of food to serve the guests. There was everything a hungry traveler could want — except bread. Whenever a guest asked for bread, Deborah felt embarrassed and ashamed. Every time she heard her father explain that the travelers in the Roman camp had bought all the bread in the city, Deborah knew that the inn could have had bread on the table if only she had been honest.

When most of the guests had gone off to bed and the inn's gate had been locked for the night, Deborah and her family washed their hands and said the dinner prayer and gathered around the table for their own meal. There were bits of spring lamb in the lentil stew. There were also olives and cheese and dates and other dried fruits. Not often was dinner so extravagant and tasty as it was tonight.

Even though the food that Deborah and Leah had prepared was as good as a rich man would have eaten, Deborah saw that Mother wasn't feeling rich or important. Mother sat back while everyone ate the stew with their fingers, scooping it from the pot with pieces of cheese because there was no bread to use for a scoop. Only occasionally did she take a bit of food for herself.

Until Andrew had pointed out how tired Mother looked, Deborah had never stopped to worry about Mother. Tonight, she saw that Mother wanted nothing so much as to sleep. She felt sorry all over again that she had been angry with her mother earlier in the day, and that she had caused trouble when Mother only needed help. She resolved that tomorrow, she would be a bigger help to both her parents. Most of all, she promised that she would never tell a lie again.

As Deborah and Leah were putting the food away before bedtime, somebody rang the big bell that hung outside the gate to the inn. The family stopped what they were doing and stared at the door, wondering who could be visiting so late at night.

It was almost dark outside. The whole world was getting ready for bed. Nobody ever came to the inn at bedtime. Deborah saw Mother mouth the word, *Who?* Father only shrugged his reply.

When Father answered the bell, Deborah followed him to see who was outside. She gasped when she saw the people who waited on the outside of the gate.

The visitors were a man and a woman and a donkey. *That* wasn't so unusual. Men and women and donkeys came to the inn all the time. But what *was* unusual was that the woman was sitting on the donkey, not the man. The woman had ridden, while the man led the donkey through the Bethlehem streets.

"Peace be with you," said the man outside the inn.

"Greetings," Father replied. He looked at the man who was on foot. Then he looked at the woman on the donkey and shook his head. Deborah was afraid Father would say something rude to the man or the lady. Even worse, she thought Father might laugh at them for putting the lady on the donkey instead of the man. But Father only stood silently at the gate, waiting for the man to speak.

"Are you the innkeeper?" The man's voice sounded tired.

"I am," Father said. "What do you want?"

"I need a place to stay," the man said. "It's just me and my wife, and our donkey."

Father snorted. "Did you just enter the city?"

"Yes," the man said. "We entered just before the city gate was closed to visitors for the night."

"Then you saw the people camped on the hillside. There are hundreds of people sleeping under the Roman tent. Why didn't you stay with them?"

The man took a deep breath and slowly let it out again. "The Romans told us the tent city was filled," he said. "They told us to come here."

"They told you wrong," Father said. "You've wasted your steps. Our inn is full. Even our courtyard is full to overflowing."

"Please," the man said. "Would it help if I told you I'm a descendant of King David? We're here for the Census."

Father laughed. "Are you crazy? This is Bethlehem. *Everyone* here is a descendant of David. That's why they've come to Bethlehem — to be counted as members of David's family. I'm even named after him: I'm David, son of David, and this is David's Inn."

"Then we're relatives," the tired man said. "My name is Joseph. Can't you find a place for us? Friend, my wife is sick. She's about to give birth, and we need a place for the child to be born."

So *that* was why the lady was on the donkey, Deborah thought. Since the lady was about to have a baby, Father would have to find room for her. But Father sighed, and Deborah knew he was going to turn the visitors away after all. She winced as her father said the words.

"No. I can't help you." Father avoided Joseph's eyes as he spoke. In Bethlehem, and throughout the whole country, the rudest thing a person could do was to refuse hospitality to another person. Father, as an innkeeper, must have been deeply humiliated. "My own wife is expecting a child, and I know I would want a place for her, but there's no place for you. Our courtyard has more people in it than animals. I'm sorry, but there's no room for anyone else."

Deborah pulled on her father's sleeve. "But there *is* a place, Father." Even in the darkness, she saw her father redden with anger, so she spoke quickly. "Under the house — nobody is staying in the cave below the house."

"That's not a cave for people," Father said gruffly. "Andrew and the other shepherds go there to eat and rest after watch. There are animals moving in and out, and people, too. It's no place for guests to stay."

"*We'll* stay there, if you'll let us," Joseph said, smiling his gratitude at Deborah. "If it's good enough for shepherds, we'll stay there gladly."

"No," Father protested. "If you stay on my property, I'm responsible for your protection. I can't protect you in a cave. If bandits come, or lions, you'll be defenseless."

"God will protect us," Joseph said. Then he and his wife and Deborah stood quietly, all of them waiting for Father to make the next move.

Father shook his head. "Bah!" he said, grumbling. "If you want to stay in a cave, so be it. Deborah, get Isaac to show them the way."

"I'll do it, Father," she said. "I know the way as well as Isaac does."

"As you wish," said Father, and he walked through the courtyard and upstairs into the house.

The man Joseph slowly turned the donkey around and led him down the hill to the cave. In all her life, Deborah had never seen a woman ride while a man walked. Deborah thought Joseph must love his wife very much if he would risk letting other people laugh at him just to make his wife feel better. Deborah decided she liked Joseph and his wife. She was glad she had reminded Father about the cave underneath the inn.

But Deborah wasn't happy for long. When they reached the cave, she felt her face turn pink with embarrassment. Even though she came here nearly every day, she had never noticed how dark and miserable the cave was.

"I'll bring you a lamp," she said to Joseph and his wife. "You can't sleep in the dark."

"We have a lamp," Joseph said, "but my wife needs something to eat and drink."

"We still have some lentil stew," Deborah said. "We don't have any bread, though. I'll bring you some stew, and some wine, and whatever else I can find."

"God will bless you for your charity," the woman said. "What is your name?"

"My name is Deborah."

"My name is Mary." Mary lowered the scarf from around her head, and Deborah saw that she was almost the same age as her own sister, Leah. She wondered if Mary dreamed of running through the hillside, the way she and Leah did. But now Mary only looked tired and ill.

"Sit down and rest," Deborah said. "I'll bring you food. You'll be safe here. My friend Andrew is a shepherd. He'll keep the robbers and the lions away from you."

"No lions or robbers will bother us, child," Joseph said. "Now that we have a place to stay, nothing can harm us."

Deborah smiled as she went to get food for Joseph and Mary. The day had begun badly, but it had ended well. Deborah hoped that the help she had given the two travelers had made up for some of the bad things she had done earlier in the day.

A Cry in the Night

When Deborah and her family went to bed that night, none of them seemed to sleep peacefully. Father snored so loudly that his rumbles and snorts kept Deborah and Leah and Mother awake. Ruth whimpered from nightmares, as she often did after a hard day at play. And Isaac tossed and changed position every few minutes.

Whenever Deborah was almost asleep, Isaac would turn over in bed and kick her in the leg. Isaac was strong, and his kicks were hard. Then Deborah would be wide awake again, trying so hard to make herself fall asleep that she only felt more awake than ever.

Finally, hours after the family had gone to bed, a strange sound filled the air.

"What's that?" Leah whispered, sounding scared.

"I don't know," Mother admitted. "Maybe it's a wolf."

Deborah didn't like the idea of wolves being so close to the inn. She snuggled closer to her mother, pushing Isaac's foot out of her side as she found the comfort of Mother's arm.

Then the sound came again.

"It's a baby!" Mother said. "Who in the neighborhood has a newborn baby?"

"I know!" Deborah whispered. "The woman who is staying in the cave below our house was expecting a baby. It must be hers."

"Then hurry!" Mother said. "If the baby was born under our roof, it's our responsibility to care for it. Take the mother a basin of water and some salt. I'll tear some cloth into swaddling strips and take them down to the cave for the new baby. Without swaddling clothes, the baby's arms and legs won't grow strong and straight."

Deborah nodded her head, yes. Then she remembered that Mother was tired and sick because she was expecting her own baby. "I'll come back for the swaddling strips," Deborah said. "Then you won't have to walk all the way down to the cave."

Mother smiled her thanks. "You're a good girl, Deborah," she said. "The swaddling clothes will be ready for you to take down when you come back."

As Mother and Leah started tearing cloth into strips, Deborah took a basin, a dish of salt, and a goatskin of water to the cave below the inn. Joseph, the husband, smiled when she approached.

"Thank you for coming," he said. "Now we have water to wash the baby and salt to toughen his skin."

"I'll bring you some swaddling strips, too," Deborah said. "Mother says you'll need to wrap the baby tightly so his arms and legs will grow straight and strong."

"Your mother is a kind woman," Joseph said when Deborah had returned with the swaddling clothes. "Would you like to see the baby?"

Deborah said, "Oh, yes."

"Mary!" Joseph called softly.   "Our visitor has brought swaddling clothes. Are you ready to show your child?"

By the dim lamplight, Deborah could see a beautiful little boy nestled into the crook of his mother's arm. "What is his name?" she asked as she approached Mary and her baby.

"His name is Jesus, and you're the first person other than Joseph and myself who has seen him." Taking the strips of cloth from Deborah, Mary smiled at the baby as she wrapped them tightly around his body.

In the dim light of the cave, with sheep and goats and the family cow milling around behind her, Deborah imagined the baby was smiling back.

When the baby was wrapped in his swaddling clothes, Deborah looked around the cave in dismay.

"What's wrong?" Joseph asked.

Deborah said, "Father was right. This is no place for a baby. There isn't even a bed for him. I wish he at least had a bed."

"He has a bed," Joseph said. "Look at this hollow in the rock, where the shepherds put straw to feed the animals. He'll be safe and warm in there."

Joseph went over and took the baby from Mary's arms. "See!" he said, placing Jesus in the niche of the rock. "It's just the right size."

"But it's a manger," Deborah protested. "Babies don't sleep in mangers."

"*This* baby sleeps in a manger," Mary said softly. "The cave is perfect. We're glad you let us stay here."

Saying goodnight to Mary and Joseph and the little baby, Deborah went back to the inn to go to sleep. She expected to find her family lying on the bed they shared, turning and tossing as they had before Jesus's cries pierced the night. Instead, she saw the whole household awake.

"Listen!" Father said when Deborah crossed the threshold. "The shepherds are driving the flocks home in the middle of the night!"

Sure enough, the sounds of bleating goats and baaing sheep rose from the streets below, waking everyone in Bethlehem who had been asleep until now. As the parade of animals and shepherds got closer, Deborah could hear Andrew and the other shepherds talking excitedly to the men who owned the animals as they dropped the animals off at each house before going on.

Soon enough, Andrew was ringing the bell at the gate of the inn. Barefooted, the family went downstairs to hear what he had to tell him.

"We saw angels!" Andrew said, before he even got inside the gate. "They sang to us in the fields, and one of them spoke to us!"

Mother paid no attention to the sheep and goats that baaed and bleated as Andrew told his news. "Why would angels come *here?*" she asked.

"It was so frightening!" Andrew admitted, ignoring Mother's question. "We didn't even *see* him walk up the hill. One moment the night was peaceful, and the next moment we heard the singing, and he was *there* on the hill with us. We wanted to run and hide, but the angel

stopped us. He told us that the Savior was born tonight
in Bethlehem. Bethlehem! Can you imagine it?"

Andrew was so excited that he didn't see the look
that Deborah exchanged with her mother and sister.
"What else did the angel say?" Leah demanded.

"He said we'd find the baby lying in a manger.
Now tell me — where would a baby be lying in a
manger?"

"*I* know!" Deborah said, almost hopping up and
down in excitement. "The baby is in the cave underneath the inn. He's lying on a straw bed in the manger,
just as the angel told you. We put the mother and father
in the cave because there was no room for them in the
inn."

"Then it *is* true," Andrew said. "I *knew* it! I'm
going to see the baby — right now, before they go
away."

Mother only shook her head. "Nobody visits a baby
before it is seven days old," she said. "Mothers and their
new babies are unclean for a week."

"Not *this* mother and baby," Andrew said. "The
angel told us to find the baby and visit him. Now — not
seven days from now. Besides, if I don't put your sheep
and your goats in the cave underneath the inn, where
else will they stay?"

Before Mother could protest, Andrew rounded up
the goats and sheep, and herded them out into the street
to take them home. Deborah could hear his cries in the
distance: "Mark! John! Bartholomew! I know where
the baby is sleeping. Come! Follow me."

When Andrew had left, Deborah and her family
returned to their house above the courtyard. As soon as

they got inside, Father sat heavily on a big chair in the corner of the room.

"The Savior was born in a cave because I wouldn't let him stay at our inn," he said sadly. "God will never forgive me for turning his parents away."

Deborah put her hand on her father's arm. "There was no place to put anyone else," she said, trying to comfort her father. But Father only looked sad. Deborah had never seen him look so guilty and miserable.

Then Isaac called everyone to the narrow window in the bedroom wall. "Look!" he said, pointing heavenward. "There's a new star in the sky!"

Father smiled as he looked at the beautiful new star. "God is good," he said. "I think He has forgiven me. This truly is a night of miracles. Let's say a prayer of thanksgiving that God has sent us his Savior, and that He found the cave under our inn worthy to be the birthplace of His son."

Deborah and her family gathered together while Father said the prayer. Then the family lay on the bed together, talking about the miracle that had come to Bethlehem this spring night. As they talked and pondered, their faces were lighted by the glow of the new star that twinkled above the inn.

The Miracle of Bethlehem

Deborah wanted to keep the Baby Jesus all to herself, but soon she realized she would have to share him with all of Bethlehem. Before the baby was two days old, it seemed as if everyone in Bethlehem had stopped by the inn to see the child that had been born in a stable. Even the people who didn't believe the story about the angel came to see the Baby Jesus anyway, just in case they were wrong. Deborah was surprised to see all the presents they brought.

Simon the Breadmaker, and all the other bakers in Bethlehem, brought loaves of bread they had made to give to the baby's mother. Potters brought pots, and winemakers brought wine, and basketmakers brought baskets, and weavers brought cloth.

So many containers of olives and grapes and dates and grain arrived that Joseph and Mary couldn't possibly have eaten everything. But Mary and Joseph thanked each giver, and showed the Baby Jesus to everyone who wanted to see him. They shared their food with everyone who came to visit.

During the daytime, Mary would often sit on the hillside near the cave and enjoy the sun and the spring breezes. People gathered around her and the Baby Jesus. Later, they went home and told each other the things that Mary and Joseph had said to them. They also told there friends about each of the baby sounds and movements that Jesus had made.

Many residents of the city — far more than could ever have been on the hillside on the night Jesus was born — told their friends they saw the angel that announced Jesus's birth. Everyone told a different story, and Andrew laughed at all of them.

"I know who was there," he said one morning, when he and Deborah's family were gathered around the breakfast table. "There were only a handful of us on the hillside that night. Everyone else is just pretending they were there so they can feel important."

"No," Mother said. "I think the others are pretending they were there because they wish they *had* been there. You were given a great blessing, Andrew, and all the people of Bethlehem want to share it."

Andrew tore off a big piece of flatbread and spread it with honey that Deborah and Leah had made. He took a big bite, being careful not to get the purple syrup all over his face. But this time, the purple goo dribbled off the bread and onto Andrew's chin. He chased the honey with his tongue, trying to clean his face, but the honey was just out of reach. Then he wiped the honey from his chin with the back of his hand, looking away as if he hoped that nobody saw the mess he had made.

Deborah covered her mouth so Andrew couldn't see the smile on her face.

At last, Andrew's chin was clean again. Then he said solemnly, "I used to think that being sold into slavery was the worst thing that ever happened to me, but now I'm glad it happened. An angel spoke to me, and I saw the Savior. I'm glad I came to Bethlehem."

"You're a wise boy," Mother said, smiling at Andrew. "Sometimes, blessings come from hardships. As angry as I was about the Census this year, now I'm glad we had it. Without the Census, the Baby Jesus would have been born someplace else."

"And the star that shines above our inn every night would be shining over another city," Father said. "I'm glad we had the Census, too. Finally — something good has come from the Romans."

But the thing that made Deborah the happiest about the Baby Jesus was not the angel or the star. Deborah was glad because she knew God had forgiven her for telling a lie. After all, God wouldn't have let the Baby Jesus be born in her father's inn if bad people lived there. Deborah made a solemn promise never to tell a lie again.

As the days passed, Deborah thought she would always have the Baby Jesus and his family living in the cave underneath her house. She thought that every afternoon when the cooling breezes came, Mary would sit on the hillside and visit with everyone who came to see her. Deborah got used to seeing the Baby Jesus wrapped so tightly in his swaddling clothes that she thought he would have the straightest arms and legs in the whole country.

But one evening, as Mother and Leah and Deborah were putting away the food after dinner, somebody rang the bell outside the inn's gate. Since nobody had ever knocked so late at night except Joseph, Deborah followed her father to the gate. Sure enough, when Father opened the gate, Joseph was standing at the threshold.

"We'll be leaving before dawn," Joseph said to Father. "I wanted to thank you for your hospitality and pay you for the food you gave to us and our donkey."

"You're leaving?" Deborah cried in dismay. "Can't you stay a little longer?"

Joseph shook his head solemnly. "No, child. We can't. Tomorrow, Jesus will be eight days old. We must take him to the temple in Jerusalem and dedicate him to the Lord."

"That's a long walk!" Deborah protested. "Jerusalem is four miles away."

"It *is* a long walk," Joseph agreed. "But the Lord has said that *every* firstborn son must be taken to the temple. We have to do what the Lord commands."

"Will you be coming back to the inn?" Deborah asked in a small voice, knowing what Joseph's answer was going to be.

"No, child," he said. "Our time here is finished. We need a home. But thank you for being our friend. We won't forget you."

Deborah had trouble sleeping that night. She wriggled around in the bed until she found a spot where she could look out the window and see the new star that was shining upon her.

At last, more than an hour before dawn, she heard the donkey's hooves clip-clopping on the stone streets of Bethlehem. Deborah climbed out of bed so she could stand at the window and watch as the donkey, piled high with gifts, found his footing on the narrow streets. She smiled when she saw that Mary was again riding the donkey. Joseph was a good man, Deborah knew. She hoped her husband would love her as much as Joseph loved Mary and Jesus.

As Joseph led the donkey toward the city gate, Deborah stood on her tiptoes so she could see them until they were out of sight. Before they turned a corner and disappeared, she raised her hand in a silent wave of farewell. But nobody saw her; the little family never looked back. Soon they were out of sight. Finally Deborah lowered her hand and crawled back into bed with her family.

Although most of the people of Bethlehem never saw Jesus again, his birth in their city was not forgotten. Often people wondered where he lived and what he was doing. They wondered when they would hear of him again.

At night, instead of going to sleep at sunset, Deborah often stayed awake just a little later than the rest of her family. As she lay in her bed looking out the window above her, she watched the new star above Bethlehem and remembered the miracle that she and all of her family had shared.